A PICTURE'S WORTH A THOUSAND SCREAMS!

SCOOBY-DOO!

FRIGHT RIDE

JOHN ROZUM
WRITER

FABIO LAGUNA
ARTIST

JOHN J. HILL
LETTERER

HEROIC AGE
COLORS

FABIO LAGUNA WITH
HEROIC AGE
COVER

HARVEY RICHARDS
EDITOR

Spotlight

visit us at www.abdopublishing.com

Reinforced library bound edition published in 2012 by Spotlight, a division of the ABDO Group, 8000 West 78th Street, Edina, Minnesota 55439. Spotlight produces high-quality reinforced library bound editions for schools and libraries. Published by agreement with Warner Bros.—A Time Warner Company. The stories, characters, and incidents mentioned are entirely fictional. All rights reserved. Used under authorization.

Printed in the United States of America, Melrose Park, Illinois.
052011
092011

Library of Congress Cataloging-in-Publication Data

Rozum, John.
  Scooby-Doo in Fright ride / writer, John Rozum ; artist, Fabio Laguna.
  -- Reinforced library bound ed.
      p. cm. -- (Scooby-Doo graphic novels)
  ISBN 978-1-59961-920-0
  1. Graphic novels. I. Laguna, Fabio, ill. II. Scooby-Doo (Television program)
III. Title. IV. Title: Fright ride.
  PZ7.7.R69Sbq 2011
  741.5'973--dc22

                            2011001368

All Spotlight books are reinforced library bindings and manufactured in the United States of America.

SCOOBY-DOO!
Table of Contents

NEW KIRK CITY DAILY NEWS

NO ONE HAS EVER BECOME A JOURNALIST BECAUSE THEY WANT TO COVER FLOWER SHOWS AND LUNCHEONS HELD BY THE LADIES' JACKHAMMER OPERATOR'S GUILD.

IF YOU WANT MORE EXCITING ASSIGNMENTS, *RYAN*, THEN YOU NEED TO GET OUT THERE AND FIND THEM FOR YOURSELF. IN THE MEANTIME I'VE GOT AN ART GALLERY OPENING...

GIVE IT TO *OGILVE*. THAT ASSIGNMENT'S A CONFLICT OF INTEREST FOR ME ANYWAY.

IF YOU WANT EXCITEMENT, CHIEF...

"...I'LL BRING YOU EXCITEMENT."

SORRY, RYAN. YOU PICKED THE WRONG WEEK TO FOLLOW US. LAST WEEK WE HAD TWO DOZEN FIRES.

THIS WEEK, NOT SO MUCH AS A CAT STUCK IN A TREE.

I DON'T KNOW WHAT TO TELL YOU, RYAN. FIVE NIGHTS WITH US AND NOT SO MUCH AS A SPEEDING TICKET TO WRITE.

NOW LAST WEEK...

UNLESS YOU WANT TO WRITE AN ARTICLE ON THE SPLINTER I'M ABOUT TO REMOVE FROM A PATIENT'S BIG TOE, YOU MIGHT WANT TO GO HOME.

I'VE NEVER SEEN THE EMERGENCY ROOM THIS EMPTY BEFORE.

≈SIGH≈ WHAT'S THIS?!

YOU WANT TO RIDE AROUND WITH THESE KIDS AND THEIR DOG?

BE REAL, HOW OFTEN CAN THESE KIDS RUN INTO MONSTERS?

EDITOR

MYSTERY, INC. NABS VILLAIN

LOCAL ARTIST SOLO SHOW TO OPEN FRIDAY

FRIGHT RIDE

SO WHAT METHODS DO YOU USE TO FIND A MYSTERY TO SOLVE?

JOHN ROZUM
WRITER

FABIO LAGUNA
ARTIST

JOHN J. HILL
LETTERER

HEROIC AGE
COLORS

FABIO LAGUNA WITH HEROIC AGE
COVER

HARVEY RICHARDS
EDITOR

TEE-HEE-HEE

RHEE-HEE-HEE

SNORT

CHUCKLE

METHODS? USUALLY THE MYSTERY MACHINE BREAKS DOWN OUTSIDE OF SOME PLACE LIKE A CREEPY MAUSOLEUM, OR WE COME ACROSS AN ARTICLE IN THE NEWSPAPER.

YOU MEAN YOU JUST STUMBLE ACROSS ALL THOSE MYSTERIES BY ACCIDENT?

I'M AFRAID SO.

BUT YOU ALWAYS TRAVEL PREPARED, RIGHT? WHAT SORT OF SPECIAL EQUIPMENT DO YOU USE? IS THIS COOLER FOR CONTAINING EVIDENCE?

NO, LIKE, THAT'S FOR STORING EMERGENCY SUPPLIES.

NOW WE'RE TALKING. EMERGENCY SUPPLIES, AND IT'S EMPTY. MUST MEAN YOU'VE HAD AN EMERGENCY, SO TELL ME ABOUT IT.

LIKE, THAT WHOLE COOLER WAS FILLED WITH ABOUT TWO DOZEN B.L.T. SANDWICHES, SIX BOTTLES OF ORANGE SODA POP, AND A GALLON OF STRAWBERRY/AVOCADO SWIRL ICE CREAM.

FOOD? SO WHAT WAS THE EMERGENCY? WERE YOU ALL TRAPPED IN THE VAN?

WAS IT OVER-TURNED IN A DITCH?

NAH, EVEN WORSE! THERE WAS FIFTEEN MINUTES UNTIL LUNCH TIME AND NOT A BURGER JOINT IN SIGHT.

SO SCOOB AND I DID WHAT ANYONE ELSE WOULD IN THAT SITUATION. WE HAD A SNACK TO TIDE US OVER. ≑HEH-HEH≑

≑SIGH≑

...ALMOST THE ENTIRE N.K.C. POLICE DEPARTMENT WAS INVOLVED IN A HIGH-SPEED CHASE TODAY WHICH ENDED IN A TREMENDOUS EXPLOSION AT THE ABANDONED CHEMICAL PLANT OUTSIDE THE CITY.

FIREFIGHTERS WORKED FOR HOURS TO CONTAIN THE BLAZE, AND THE HOSPITAL EMERGENCY ROOMS WERE OVERRUN BY PEOPLE BROUGHT IN TO BE TREATED FOR INHALING THE FUMES...

The next day a tantalizing mystery fell right into their laps. It was right out of the headlines, just the way Velma Dinkley told me some of their most challenging mysteries presented themselves.

They were eager to take the case. It was fascinating to see the gears churning in the minds of these celebrated sleuths as they began to process the mystery, even before a single clue presented itself.

SO? IT'S A PAINTING OF A MONSTER.

LOOK AT IT. THE FEATURED ARTIST CLAIMS SHE DIDN'T PAINT IT. IT DOESN'T LOOK ANYTHING LIKE HER OTHER WORK. NO ONE KNOWS HOW IT GOT HERE.

IT HAS A MONSTER IN IT.

IT'S MYSTERIOUS ALL RIGHT.

IT'S JUST NOT OUR KIND OF MYSTERY.

The next day I met with the members of Mystery, Inc. at their base, where they were working out their approach to the mystery of the monster painting, as this case would later be known.

HAVE YOU SEEN THIS ITEM IN TODAY'S PAPER?

IT'S STILL NOT OUR KIND OF MYSTERY.

THOUGH IT'S A LITTLE CLOSER.

VALUABLE STATUE STOLEN

Little did anyone know, but the next day, the mystery would become even more baffling.

NOW IT'S OUR KIND OF MYSTERY.

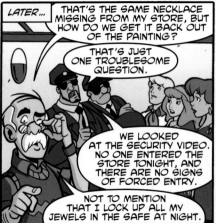

GREAT! WE CHIPPED THE FRAME.

HELP ME HANG IT BACK UP. MAYBE NO ONE WILL NOTICE.

THUNK

I GUESS WE'D BETTER GO SEE WHAT THAT NOISE IS.

Despite all their thoroughness and determination, I was beginning to get the sense that these kids were just going in circles...

≥WHEW!≤ IT'S JUST THE OTHERS CHECKING FOR SECRET PANELS.

RAGGY!

...that they didn't have any clue when it came to this strange mystery which was happening in their very presence.

THE MONSTER'S SKEDADDLED AGAIN!

QUICK, EVERYONE! FAN OUT! HE'S GOT TO BE HERE SOMEWHERE!

In spite of their presence...

THE FRONT DOOR'S STILL LOCKED AND THE DOOR ALARM IS STILL ON.

...almost taunting them from under their very noses.

EXIT

SAME FOR THE BACK DOOR.

THAT LEAVES THE BASEMENT.

CLICK

LIKE, NEVER MIND THE BASEMENT, OLD GOON FACE IS BACK IN THE PAINTING.

THIS TIME HE HAS A... *MAGAZINE?*

NOT JUST *ANY* MAGAZINE, BUT THE *RARE FIRST ISSUE* OF "VAULT OF MONSTERS!"

DO YOU HAVE ANY IDEA HOW MUCH THAT'S WORTH? HE MUST HAVE SWIPED IT FROM THAT COMIC BOOK STORE DOWN THE STREET.

When this mystery began, I admired Fred Jones's quick thinking and take-action persona, but now I began to wonder if perhaps...

...he was keeping the team moving to hide the fact that he had no idea where to go with this case more than he was leading them to a solution.

ALL THE MORE REASON TO CHECK THE BASEMENT. ALL OF THE STOLEN ITEMS IN THE PAINTING CAME FROM STORES ON THIS BLOCK.

IF THEY'RE NOT CONNECTED FROM THE ROOFTOPS, THEN MAYBE THEY'RE CONNECTED DOWN HERE.

THESE WALLS ARE ALL SOLID.

THERE'S A DRAINAGE PIPE WHICH RUNS UNDER THE STORES ON THIS SIDE OF THE STREET, BUT I DOUBT EVEN OUR TWO-DIMENSIONAL MONSTER COULD SQUEEZE THROUGH THAT GRATE.

I'M BAFFLED. WE'RE NOT ANY BETTER OFF THAN WE WERE WHEN THIS MYSTERY STARTED.

I WOULDN'T SAY THAT. WE'VE RULED A LOT OF THINGS OUT. ENOUGH THAT I HAVE SOME IDEAS IN MIND FOR WHEN WE COME BACK TOMORROW.

The next night, we were back inside the gallery for another vigil, locked in with a monster that could come and go at will, while we could only wonder "how?"

THAT DIDN'T TAKE LONG. WE WEREN'T EVEN IN JULIE'S OFFICE FOR FIVE MINUTES WHILE SHE LOCKED UP FOR THE NIGHT, AND ALREADY THE MONSTER'S ON THE LOOSE.

BUT NOW, WE'LL KNOW HOW IT'S GETTING IN AND OUT.

WHAT ARE YOU DOING?

I'M POURING A THIN LAYER OF FLOUR ACROSS THE GALLERY FLOOR. WHEN THE MONSTER RETURNS WE'LL BE ABLE TO SEE HOW IT GOT IN.

BUT WHAT ABOUT SHAGGY AND SCOOBY? WON'T THEY MESS UP THE FLOUR WHEN THEY COME IN?

FIRST OF ALL, THEY CAN'T GET BACK IN SINCE JULIE HAS TURNED ON THE ALARMS TO THE DOORS, AND SECONDLY, THEY'RE KEEPING BUSY WITH AN ASSIGNMENT OF THEIR OWN.

WHAT ASSIGNMENT?

YOU'LL KNOW SOON ENOUGH.

SHHH. I HEAR SOMETHING.

THE MONSTER'S BACK!

YES, AND IT'S LEFT BEHIND THE DAINTIEST, MOST UNMONSTER-LIKE FOOTPRINTS I'VE EVER SEEN.

IT'S A WOMAN'S SHOE! IT LOOKS LIKE A SLIPPER.

YES, AND NOTICE HOW THE TRACKS HEAD BACK OUT OF THE GALLERY AS WELL.

NOT ONLY THAT, BUT THEY STOP AND FACE THE ALARM BOX IN EACH DIRECTION.

TO DEACTIVATE AND ACTIVATE THE ALARM, YOU MEAN?

PRECISELY.

I'LL BET THEY'RE A GOOD MATCH FOR THE FLOUR-COVERED VELVET SLIPPERS JULIE'S WEARING.

LIKE NO WONDER WE NEVER HEARD ANYONE COMING OR GOING. THOSE THINGS DON'T MAKE A SOUND.

DING DING DING DING DING DING

YOU'VE JUST SET OFF THE ALARM, NOW THE COPS WILL COME!

I'M SURE THE POLICE WILL BE INTERESTED IN HEARING THE STORY YOU AND JULIE HAVE TO TELL THEM.

DING DING DING

ME? WHAT DO I HAVE TO DO WITH ANY OF THIS?

GIVE IT A REST, RYAN. IT'S OVER.

FOR ONE THING, JULIE'S YOUR SISTER.

SHAGGY, WOULD YOU CARE TO SHARE WHAT YOU AND SCOOBY-DOO FOUND OUT?

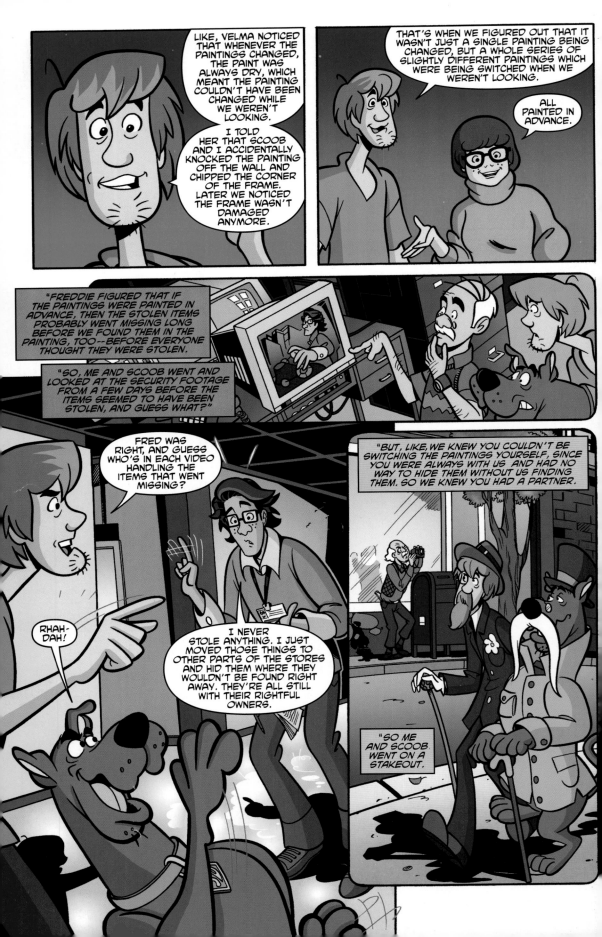

LIKE, VELMA NOTICED THAT WHENEVER THE PAINTINGS CHANGED, THE PAINT WAS ALWAYS DRY, WHICH MEANT THE PAINTING COULDN'T HAVE BEEN CHANGED WHILE WE WEREN'T LOOKING.

I TOLD HER THAT SCOOB AND I ACCIDENTALLY KNOCKED THE PAINTING OFF THE WALL AND CHIPPED THE CORNER OF THE FRAME. LATER WE NOTICED THE FRAME WASN'T DAMAGED ANYMORE.

THAT'S WHEN WE FIGURED OUT THAT IT WASN'T JUST A SINGLE PAINTING BEING CHANGED, BUT A WHOLE SERIES OF SLIGHTLY DIFFERENT PAINTINGS WHICH WERE BEING SWITCHED WHEN WE WEREN'T LOOKING.

ALL PAINTED IN ADVANCE.

"FREDDIE FIGURED THAT IF THE PAINTINGS WERE PAINTED IN ADVANCE, THEN THE STOLEN ITEMS PROBABLY WENT MISSING LONG BEFORE WE FOUND THEM IN THE PAINTING, TOO--BEFORE EVERYONE THOUGHT THEY WERE STOLEN."

"SO, ME AND SCOOB WENT AND LOOKED AT THE SECURITY FOOTAGE FROM A FEW DAYS BEFORE THE ITEMS SEEMED TO HAVE BEEN STOLEN, AND GUESS WHAT?"

FRED WAS RIGHT, AND GUESS WHO'S IN EACH VIDEO HANDLING THE ITEMS THAT WENT MISSING?

RHAH-DAH!

I NEVER STOLE ANYTHING. I JUST MOVED THOSE THINGS TO OTHER PARTS OF THE STORES AND HID THEM WHERE THEY WOULDN'T BE FOUND RIGHT AWAY. THEY'RE ALL STILL WITH THEIR RIGHTFUL OWNERS.

"BUT, LIKE, WE KNEW YOU COULDN'T BE SWITCHING THE PAINTINGS YOURSELF, SINCE YOU WERE ALWAYS WITH US AND HAD NO WAY TO HIDE THEM WITHOUT US FINDING THEM. SO WE KNEW YOU HAD A PARTNER."

"SO ME AND SCOOB WENT ON A STAKEOUT."

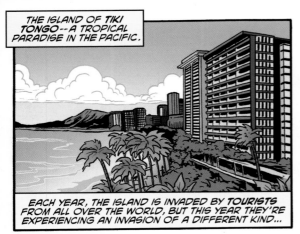

THE ISLAND OF TIKI TONGO--A TROPICAL PARADISE IN THE PACIFIC.

EACH YEAR, THE ISLAND IS INVADED BY TOURISTS FROM ALL OVER THE WORLD, BUT THIS YEAR THEY'RE EXPERIENCING AN INVASION OF A DIFFERENT KIND...

DUDE! THIS ISLAND HAS NEVER SEEN ANYTHING LIKE THE *INTERNATIONAL SURF OPEN!* CHECK OUT ALL THE *MEDIA!*

2009 INTERNATIONAL SURF OPEN

TOTAL *SENSORY OVERLOAD!* DUDE, LET'S GET OUT OF HERE AND GET SOME *FOOD!*

ONE PRIVATE *PICNIC* COMING RIGHT UP, BRO!

LOOKS LIKE WE GOT THE *CAMP GROUNDS* ALL TO OURSELVES! SWEET!

KINDA *SPOOKY*, NOBODY BEING HERE. WHERE'D EVERYBODY GO?

THEY'RE CATCHING SOME *WAVES*, DUMMY! YOU DON'T THINK THEY WERE *SCARED OFF* BY A--

--A *GHOST?*

INTERLOPERS! INTRUDERS! OUTSIDERS ARE NOT WELCOME ON *TIKI TONGO!*

BEGONE... OR FACE THE *WRATH* OF THE GREAT *WARRIOR CHIEF!*

In the Spirit

FRANK STROM - WRITER
SCOTT NEELY - ARTIST
HEROIC AGE - COLOR
JOHN J. HILL - LETTERER
HARVEY RICHARDS - EDITOR

I *KNEW* IT! I KNEW THERE'D BE *TROUBLE* WITH ALL THIS MEDIA HOOPLA!

TOO MANY *REPORTERS!* TOO MUCH *CRAZINESS!*

BUT, CONSTABLE, WE *WEREN'T* ATTACKED BY *REPORTERS.*

YEAH! IT WAS A...A...A *NATIVE WARRIOR SPIRIT* OR SOMETHING!

TERRIFIC. I'VE GOT *ENOUGH* WORK ON MY HANDS WITHOUT DEALING WITH A *GHOST SCAM!*

NOT TO WORRY, CONSTABLE--*MYSTERY, INC.* IS ON THE JOB!

AND WHERE DID YOU MEET THIS *WARRIOR SPIRIT,* GUYS?

WELL, WE WERE KINDA TRESPASSING ON THE *CAMP GROUNDS*--!

TRESPASSING?!?

SETTLE DOWN. THEY DIDN'T MEAN ANY HARM.

HMM. I'D LIKE TO SNOOP AROUND THE PLACE MYSELF, IF THAT'S OKAY.

THAT CAN BE *ARRANGED...* NOT THAT I EXPECT YOU'LL *FIND* ANYTHING!

THESE ARE *PRIVATELY OWNED* CABINS THAT ARE RENTED OUT TO *TOURISTS*. WITH THE STUPID *SURFING CONTEST* GOING ON, THE PLACE IS *PACKED*.

WEIRD! THEN HOW COME IT'S, LIKE, A *GHOST* TOWN?

IMPOSSIBLE! THE CABINS CAN'T *ALL* BE DESERTED!

THERE'S ONLY ONE WAY TO FIND OUT--!

LET'S *SPLIT UP* AND HAVE A LOOK, GANG. AND IF YOU *DO* FIND ANYONE, REMEMBER TO BE *POLITE!*

HEY-- ME AND SCOOBY ARE *ALWAYS* POLITE!

WE'LL POLITELY HELP OURSELVES TO ANY *FOOD* THAT WAS, LIKE, LEFT BEHIND! RIGHT, SCOOB?

RRREAH RREAH RRREAH!

AFTER ALL, WE *ARE* GUESTS, AND IF NO ONE'S HOME--?

TRESPASSERS!

YOIKS! THE S-S-S-*SPIRIT WARRIOR*!!!

SHAGGY?

I GOT A FEELING SOMEONE WASN'T EXPECTING COMPANY!

INVADERS! THE BORDERS OF *TIKI TONGO* ARE *CLOSED* TO OUTSIDERS!

ALL UNWELCOME *INTRUDERS* ON THIS ISLAND WILL FACE *DESTRUCTION*--

--AT THE HANDS OF THE GREAT *WARRIOR CHIEF!*

FA-SHOOOM!

FIRE OUT OF *NOWHERE!* LIKE *MAGIC!*

THAT'S NOT THE *ONLY* MAGIC TRICK. CHECK IT OUT--THE SPIRIT WARRIOR *VANISHED* INTO THE GREAT BEYOND!

HE EITHER COMMANDS POWERFUL *MYSTIC FORCES*...OR A WELL-PLACED *TRAPDOOR!*

CALM DOWN, SHAGGY--THE GHOUL IS *GONE.* AT LEAST FOR *NOW.*

OH, MAN! I WAS SO *SCARED* I ALMOST LOST MY *APPETITE!*

THAT'S *GOTTA* BE AN *EXAGGER-ATION!*

WHAT TH--? ARE YOU KIDS *OKAY?* WHAT *HAPPENED?*

WE GOT A FIRSTHAND LOOK AT THE *SPIRIT WARRIOR,* WHO SEEMED PRETTY *AUTHENTIC* ...RIGHT DOWN TO THE *ANTIQUE JEWELRY* HE WAS WEARING.

CONSTABLE, ARE THERE ANY *EXPERTS* ON ISLAND *HISTORY?*

I KNOW JUST THE MAN-- THE LOCAL *SHAMAN!*

KING TONGO--HE WAS THE FIRST *RULER* OF TIKI TONGO.

HE WAS INDEED A MIGHTY *WARRIOR* AND A FIERCE *PROTECTOR* OF HIS PEOPLE.

HE WAS FAMOUS FOR DRIVING *FOREIGNERS* FROM THE ISLAND. MOST CERTAINLY HE WOULD *NOT* BE *HAPPY* WITH ALL THE *TOURISTS* WE SEE TODAY!

ROYAL ARTIFACTS FROM THAT PERIOD ARE HARD TO COME BY, BUT THE INSTITUTE HAS A FAIRLY GOOD COLLECTION.

IN THAT CASE, SIR, *YOU* MUST BE OUR SO-CALLED *SPIRIT,* AS YOU'RE THE ONLY PERSON WITH ACCESS TO THIS *JEWELRY!*

I'M NOT SO *SURE* ABOUT THAT. THERE MIGHT BE... ER...SOMEONE *ELSE* WITH A NICE JEWELRY COLLECTION--!

WHAT ARE YOU SAYING? WE HAVE THE OBVIOUS *CULPRIT* IN OUR HANDS!

A LITTLE *TOO* OBVIOUS FOR ME. I'D LIKE TO CONTINUE THE *INVESTIGATION.*

YO, SHAGGY-DUDE! YOU READY TO *PARTY*?

PARTY?

TOTAL *SHINDIG!* GIRLS, GAMES AND *BARBECUE!*

FREE EATS?!? SOUNDS *GREAT,* BUT AREN'T YOU WORRIED ABOUT THE *SPIRIT WARRIOR?*

WE KNOW A *SECRET COVE!* SHAGGY-DUDE, HE WILL *NEVER* FIND US!

SHORTLY...

RRR'OH BOY! RRRARBECUE! RRRUMMY-RRRUM-RRRUM!

FIRST THINGS FIRST, SCOOBY-DOO. WE GOTTA, LIKE, *LOCATE* THE PARTY BEFORE WE CAN *EAT!*

LUCKY FOR US, THE GUYS GAVE US *SECRET DIRECTIONS* TO THE *SECRET COVE*, OR WE'D BE, LIKE, HOPELESSLY *LOST* AND THAT AIN'T NO SECRET!

WATCH YOUR *STEP*, SCOOB. YOU NEVER KNOW WHAT *NASTY THING* YOU MIGHT RUN INTO OUT HERE--!

FOOLS! YOU DARE IGNORE MY *WARNINGS*?

Y-Y-*YOIKS*!!! WOULD YOU BELIEVE WE'RE HARD OF HEARING--?

LOOK OUT! MAD GHOST ON THE *RAMPAGE!* HELP!!!

ALL OUTSIDERS WILL BE PUNISHED!!

CAN AN *HISTORIC* TRIBAL CHIEF SET *CURRENT* LAWS?

I DUNNO, BUT WE DON'T HAVE TIME FOR THE *LAWYERS* TO FIGURE IT OUT!

SHAGGY, SCOOBY--*INCOMING!*

WHADDYA KNOW-- *UNIDENTIFIED FLYING HOT DOGS!* A CLOSE ENCOUNTER OF THE *BEST* KIND!

MMM-RRREAH!

F-WOOOOM

THWUMP

SPLORSH

I SURE HOPE WE DON'T GET *FINED* FOR FISHING WITHOUT A *LICENSE!*

NOT TO WORRY-- OUR FRIEND THE *SPIRIT WARRIOR* WILL LET US OFF WITH A *WARNING!*

HOW'S THAT? IF HE'S REALLY THE *INSTITUTE PROFESSOR*--?

NOPE! UNLESS I MISS MY GUESS, HE'S REALLY THE *CONSTABLE!* I SPOTTED HIM WEARING AN ANTIQUE *BRACELET* SIMILAR TO THE OTHER JEWELRY.

I FIGURED HE MUST BE A DISTANT *DESCENDANT* OF THE REAL *KING TONGO!*

YOU NOSY KIDS THINK YOU KNOW EVERYTHING! YOU'RE WRONG!

MY GREAT RELATIVE WOULD WANT HIS ISLAND'S HISTORY PROTECTED FROM SOMETHING AS *TASTELESS* AS A *SURFING COMPETITION!*

I DUNNO ABOUT THE SURFING COMPETITION, BUT THE HOT DOGS ARE AS *TASTEFUL* AS IT GETS!

RRRROOBY-RRROOBY-RRROO!

THE END!